59372088821627   FTBC

D0601440

GRANDMA in BLUE with RED HAT

WORDS BY SCOTT MENCHIN   PICTURES BY HARRY BLISS

ABRAMS BOOKS FOR YOUNG READERS, NEW YORK

FOR KARINA'S
GRANDMA, OLGA
—S.M.

FOR TOM BLISS
—H.B.

The illustrations in this book were made with
pen and ink and then colored with watercolor.

Library of Congress Cataloging-in-Publication Data

Menchin, Scott.
Grandma in blue with red hat / words by Scott Menchin ;
illustrated by Harry Bliss.
pages cm
Summary: After his teacher says that anything can be in an art exhibition,
and his fellow students give myriad reasons why something might belong
in a museum, a child offers his special grandmother as an exhibit but
when the curator cites a rule against accepting grandmas, the child has
a better idea.
ISBN 978-1-4197-1484-9
[1. Art—Fiction. 2. Museums—Fiction. 3. Grandmothers—Fiction.]
I. Bliss, Harry, 1964- illustrator. II. Title.
PZ7.M522Gr 2015
[E]—dc23
2014015928

Text copyright © 2015 Scott Menchin
Illustrations copyright © 2015 Harry Bliss
Book design by Chad W. Beckerman

Published in 2015 by Abrams Books for Young Readers, an imprint of
ABRAMS. All rights reserved. No portion of this book may be reproduced,
stored in a retrieval system, or transmitted in any form or by any means,
mechanical, electronic, photocopying, recording, or otherwise, without
written permission from the publisher.

Printed and bound in China
10 9 8 7 6 5 4 3 2 1

Abrams Books for Young Readers are available at special discounts when
purchased in quantity for premiums and promotions as well as fundraising
or educational use. Special editions can also be created to specification. For
details, contact specialsales@abramsbooks.com or the address below.

ABRAMS
THE ART OF BOOKS SINCE 1949

115 West 18th Street
New York, NY 10011
www.abramsbooks.com

Saturday is the best day. Because that's the day I go to art class at the museum.

I have been coming here forever.

Ms. Montebello is the art teacher. She knows everything about art.

DID YOU KNOW THAT *ANYTHING* CAN BE IN AN ART EXHIBITION? TOYS. HAIR CLIPS. GUITARS. WATER BOTTLES. ANYTHING!

Ms. Montebello calls us her little Picassos. Picasso was a famous artist. He liked to paint in his underwear.

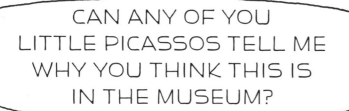

That's the question Ms. Montebello always asks us when we look at art.

Alice says,

BECAUSE IT'S BEAUTIFUL.

Sasha says,

Henry says,

BECAUSE IT TELLS A STORY.

Thomas says,

Jack says,

BECAUSE IT
MAKES ME
FEEL GOOD.

Alex says,

Karina says,

BECAUSE THERE'S ONLY ONE LIKE IT IN THE WHOLE WORLD.

Ms. Montebello says there are no wrong answers when it comes to art, and she explains that most of the artwork was given to the museum.

MAYBE SOMEDAY I COULD GIVE SOME ARTWORK TO THE MUSEUM!

Grandma is waiting for me at home.

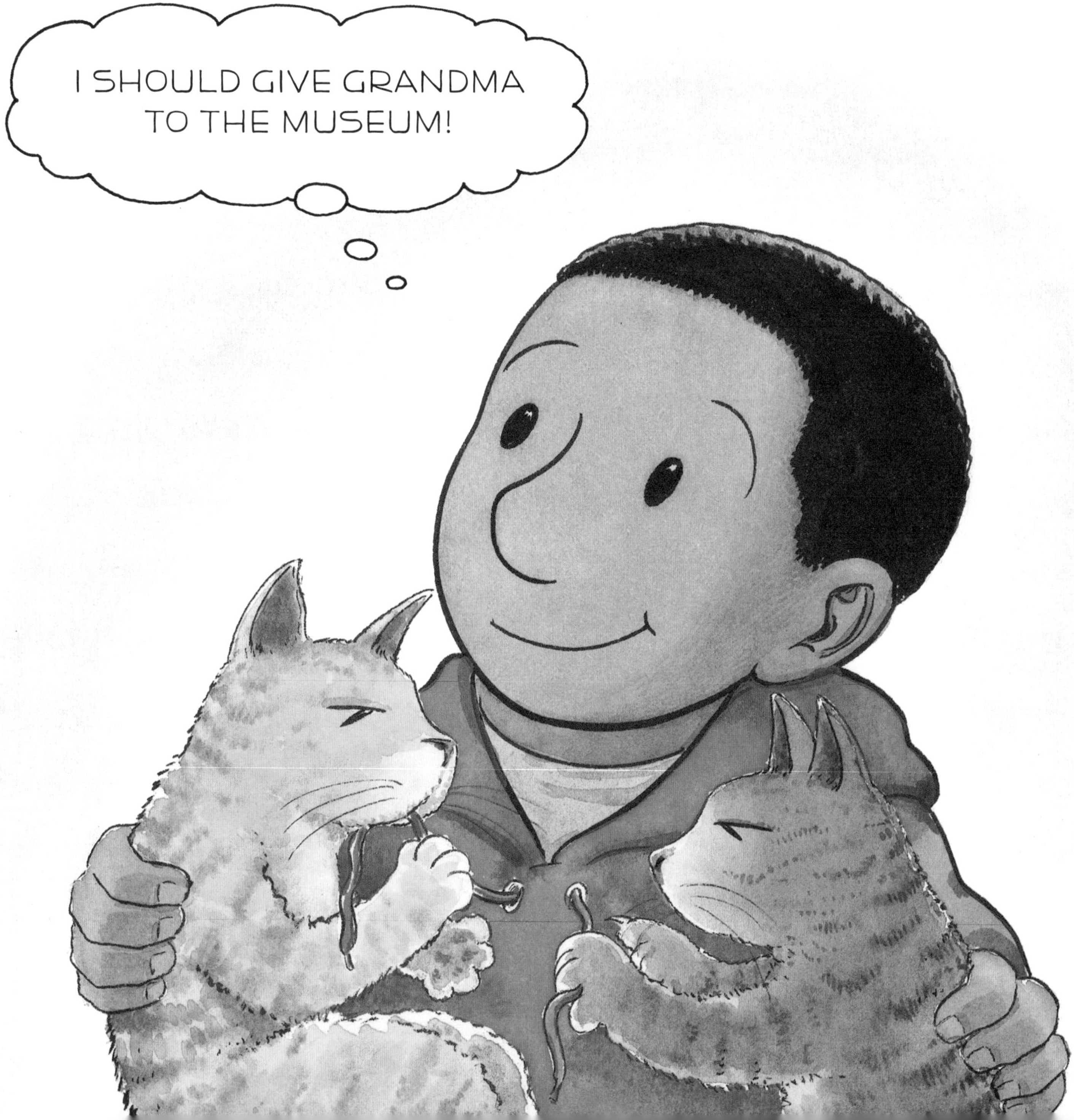
I SHOULD GIVE GRANDMA TO THE MUSEUM!

The next week, I tell Ms. Montebello about my idea, and she tells me I should ask the curator of the museum.

And that's when I have a great idea.

Mom and Dad and Grandma help me get ready for the big day.

My friends are there.
Grandma's friends are there.
Mom and Dad's friends are there.
And Ms. Montebello and the curator are there!

Just like Grandma.